shar-dey

Fee-bee

Kwah-mey

FROY-LIN

Jahng lee

Yung

Wah-KEEN

la-KEE-sha

My name is Wakawakaloch!

(wa-ka-wa-ka-lokh—with a throat-clearing "ch" at the end)

Words by Chana Stiefel
Pictures by Mary Sullivan

Houghton Mifflin Harcourt
Boston   New York

To all the Chanas —C.S.

To Susie —M.S.

The illustrations in this book were digitally drawn and colored.
The text type was set in Shaky Hand Some Comic and Stone Hinge Pro.
The display type was hand lettered by Mary Sullivan.

Library of Congress Cataloging-in-Publication Data is on file.
ISBN: 978-1-328-73209-5
Manufactured in China
SCP 10 9 8 7 6 5 4 3 2 1
4500760854

Wakawakaloch was in a volcanic mood.

Everyone was bungling her name.

"Roll boulder faster, Walawala!" shouted Oog.

"That not my name!" grumbled Wakawakaloch.

At Sabertooth Safety Class . . .

"Look out, Wammabammaslamma!" hollered Boog.

"That NOT my name!" seethed Wakawakaloch.

During Club Club . . .

"Swing, Lokamokatok!" cheered Goog.

"THAT! NOT! MY! NAME!"

exploded Wakawakaloch.

And she smashed her club to smithereens.

WHAM!
BAM!
SLAM!

"Why so cranky, sweet child?" asked Ma.
"Me changing my name to Gloop!" said Wakawakaloch.

"Gloop good name," said Pa.
"But Wakawakaloch
in family many, many
moons."

"**No one says it right,**" sobbed Wakawakaloch.

"**And me never find T-shirt with my name on it.**"

"**What are shirt tees?**" asked Ma.

"**Me think girl has lost her pebbles,**" said Pa.

"**We must bring her to Elder Mooch.**"

Elder Mooch looked as old as a weather-beaten tetrapod and smelled like rotting mammoth poop.

But he was still the wisest Neanderthal in the village.

"Tell me troubles, dear Wamawamabloch," said Elder Mooch.

"Me Wakawakaloch!" she cried.

"Just pulling your leg," Elder Mooch chuckled.

"Me want easy name like Oog, Boog, and Goog," whimpered Wakawakaloch. "A name you find on T-shirt."

"**Me see,**" said Elder Mooch. "**The problem, my dear, is that you are forward thinker. You must be backwards seer too.**"

Wakawakaloch had no idea what Elder Mooch meant, but she paid him two skinny pigeons and stomped back to her cave.

That night, while her family snored,
Wakawakaloch tossed and turned.
She thought about Elder Mooch's
message. What did it mean
to be a forward thinker and
a backwards seer?

As the fire's flames flickered and danced on the cave's walls,
images suddenly became clear.

There was the Mighty Wakawakaloch, her great-great-great-great-great-grandmother, performing brave and heroic acts.

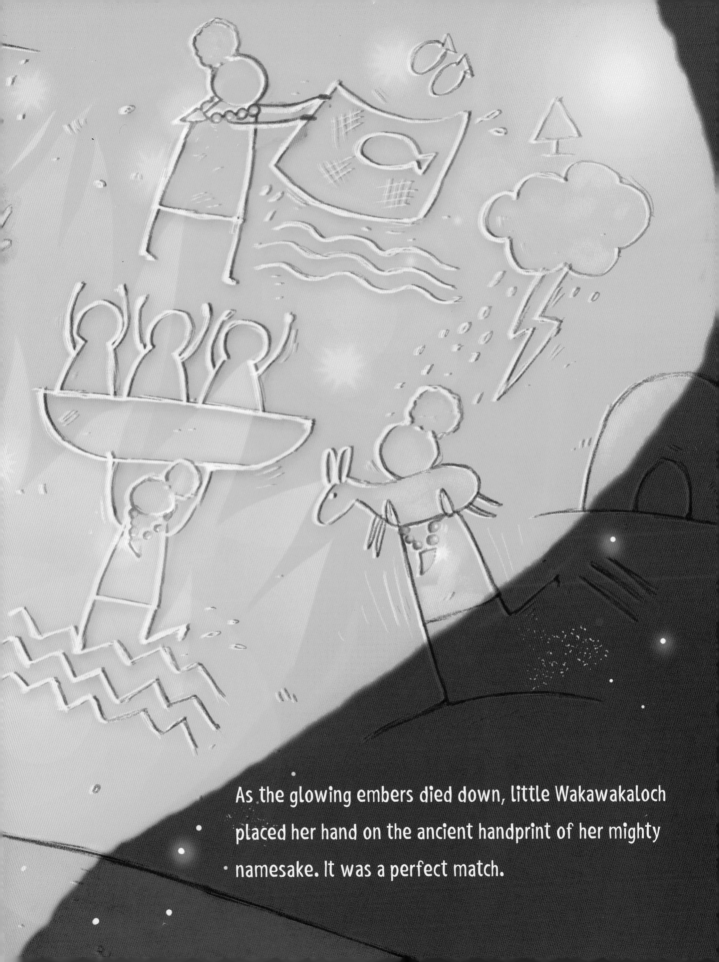

As the glowing embers died down, little Wakawakaloch placed her hand on the ancient handprint of her mighty namesake. It was a perfect match.

"Good morning, Gloop!" said Pa.
"Me not Gloop," said his daughter.
"Me Wakawakaloch,
    backwards seer and
    forward thinker."

"What you seeing?" asked Pa.

"And thinking?" asked Ma.

"Me see my name is mighty, like **Great-Great-Great-Great-Great-Grandmother**," said Wakawakaloch.

"And me think I can use my name to help others."

At the next Roll-the-Boulder tournament,
Wakawakaloch had an earthshaking idea.

"Ooga booga, Wakawakaloch!"
said Oog, Goog, and Boog.

(That means "Way cool!")

"Three T-shirts, please," said Elder Mooch.

"No charge," winked Wakawakaloch.

"You have shirt that says 'Hoopaloopie'?"

asked a little boy.

"Not yet," said Wakawakaloch. "But me have one ready in two shakes of sabertooth tail."

Siobhan

Shiv-ahn

Deandre

dee-ON-dray

Noël

No-el

Sean

Shawn

Ximena

Hee-meh-na

Xavier

ZAYV-yer

Chana

Kh-ah-nah—
(with a throat
clearing "ch" at
the beginning)

Noam

No-Ahm